FROSTING FATALITY

RAISED AND GLAZED COZY MYSTERIES,
BOOK 34

EMMA AINSLEY

SUMMER PRESCOTT BOOKS PUBLISHING

CHAPTER ONE

"Tell me again where the two of you are going this afternoon," Ruby Cobb asked her best friend and business partner, Maggie Mission, owner of Dogwood Donuts. She leaned against the prep table and folded her arms over her dirty apron.

"A yard sale," Maggie said, shrugging her shoulders slightly. She failed to see the issue with leaving work a little early. "Haven't you ever been to a yard sale before?"

"Don't you mean someone getting rid of the junk in their attic sale?" Orson Hawley grumbled from his seat in the corner. Despite the fact that his employment with the donut shop had ended several months ago, he often found himself in the middle of kitchen conversations offering his curmudgeonly perspective.

"I don't know why you have such a bad outlook on everything," Naomi Gardner chastised him from her station near the automatic donut maker. She held a large mixing bowl over the batter hopper as she spoke. "Yard sales are a big deal around these parts. Don't tell me you've never wanted to stop by and check out what deals you could find."

"That answer would be no," Orson said. "There is no good reason in the world to stop at a yard sale. All you're doing is picking up cheap junk."

"You know what they say," Myra Sawyer Macklin, another longtime member of the donut shop staff, said. "One man's junk is another man's treasure."

"I think Orson's just upset we didn't invite him to go with us," Maggie teased. She rolled a large piece of dough over and over and sealed the ends. She smiled at him as she cut through the dough and placed the cinnamon rolls on a sheet pan to rise.

"I don't think there's anything particularly wrong with yard sales," Ruby continued. "They've just never been something I go out of my way for. I've never known you to do that either, Maggie."

"I'm a huge yard sale fan," Naomi said. She finished pouring the batter into the doughnut maker and turned it on for the next batch. "Maggie is going with me this time because she's in search of a few things for Wyatt."

"What does Wyatt need?" Orson asked, perking up suddenly. In addition to being the resident curmudgeon, Orson also fulfilled the very important role of resident grandpa to Maggie's own grandson, Wyatt, and Myra's daughter, Lexi. "If that boy needs something, why haven't you let me know?"

"He doesn't need anything specifically," Maggie said. "It's just that Bradley has expressed a desire to find a more suitable bed for him. I told him I'd look for a bed frame at a yard sale because Wyatt may outgrow it sooner than we think, and we'd just need to buy another one anyway."

"You see," Naomi said. "Sometimes yard sales do make sense. Why should Bradley spend a bunch of money if he doesn't need to?"

"I get it," Ruby said. She turned back to the prep table and began slicing apples for her famous apple slaw.

"Dogwood Mountain advertised their citywide yard sale for this weekend, and I decided to take a look and see what I could find," Maggie said, explaining it once more. "It's the busiest yard sale weekend of the year. People reserve their best stuff to put out during this weekend. I figured it won't hurt to at least look."

"And the sale we're going to advertised various pieces of furniture," Naomi explained, as if they needed to justify their excursion even more.

"You know, if you find they have a lot, you'll have to let me know," Myra said. "Lexi could use a new dresser. It seems like every time I do laundry, her clothes seem to multiply. I'm running out of room to put everything."

"Then why don't we go to the store and look for a new dresser?" Orson asked, throwing his hands up in the air. "I've got news for you girls. Another man's junk is just junk. There's no treasure involved."

"Haven't you heard of reduce, recycle, reuse?" Naomi asked. "If someone no longer needs a good dresser, why should it go into a landfill?"

"Why not just keep it?" Orson said.

"Because sometimes people downsize," Myra said. "Or maybe they want new furniture, and they have to get rid of their old furniture somewhere."

"There you go," Orson said, snapping his fingers in Myra's direction.

"There I go, meaning what exactly?" Myra said.

"Why can't people just be satisfied with what they have?" Orson folded his arms over his chest.

"Wait a minute," Ruby said. "Let me see if I have this straight. It's not yard sales you have an issue with, it's that you think everyone should just keep what they already have, rather than going out and buying more?"

"Something like that," Orson said. "If it wasn't for the need to go out and buy new things every five years, there'd be no need for yard sales. We'd all just keep what we already have and be done with it."

"But what's the matter with redecorating your house once in a while?" Naomi asked. "I certainly wouldn't expect someone nowadays to have the same furniture and decor they had thirty years ago."

"Don't you see? It's nothing more than a racket. People go on those home improvement shows and tell everybody that this is in style and that's outdated, so people will go out and spend all their money buying more. Then they'll have the old stuff to deal with and it's ridiculous. Just keep what you have, throw a fresh coat of paint on it, and be satisfied."

"You are too much sometimes." Maggie placed the last pan of cinnamon rolls on the warming rack and headed for the sink to wash the sticky dough off her hands.

Orson huffed. "I'm not the one going out to spend

money on an old bed for a little boy who deserves brand new."

"Orson Hawley," Maggie said, tossing a towel in his direction. "You take that back right now. You make it sound like I wouldn't do anything for that little boy."

"Then why are you buying a bed he's only going to use for a year or two?" Orson asked. "Why not go out and buy him the furniture he'll have through the rest of his childhood?"

"Because he's still a little small for that," Maggie said. "And besides, Bradley doesn't want to get him anything that big right now." Her eyes twinkled as she spoke. She was bursting with news that she knew was not hers to share, but she wanted so badly to share it anyway.

"You're just going to have to throw that smaller bed in the trash anyway when he starts school," Orson continued. "Why not just get him a regular bed with guardrails or something?"

"Because." Maggie grinned. "Maybe Bradley plans to hang on to that smaller bed instead of getting rid of it."

"Why would he do that?" Ruby asked. "Unless he plans to have more children someday."

"I guess that's always a possibility," Maggie said, her voice practically singing.

"Wait a minute," Ruby said suddenly. She threw her paring knife down on the prep table and planted her hands on her hips. "Is there something you're not telling us? Maybe a big announcement that you're holding back?"

"Oh, my goodness," Myra said, clasping her hand over her mouth.

"What is it?" Naomi asked.

"Are you trying to tell us you're about to be a grandmother again?" Myra asked, removing her hand from her mouth.

"A grandmother again? Oh, no," Maggie said quickly, blushing wildly. "Bradley's not expecting another baby."

"Then why is he thinking ahead to more chil-dren?" Orson asked. For the moment, his focus shifted from the crime of yard sales shopping to Bradley's future. "That woman he's been seeing is wonderful, but it hasn't been very long."

"Well, I mean, Bradley is still a young man," Maggie said defensively. "He has his entire life ahead of him to think about."

"Yes, but people don't usually think about things

like that unless they're making plans for their future," Ruby said. "Come to think of it, Bradley sent me a text yesterday asking me to meet him for lunch next week. It's not terribly unusual, but it was unexpected."

"All right, Maggie," Naomi said. "Out with it. What's going on?"

"I am not at liberty to say anything," she said decisively.

"So, there is something going on?" Myra asked. "Bradley has some big news to share. Is that it?"

"Nope, I'm not going to say a word," Maggie said, pretending to button her lips.

"Then maybe we can guess," Naomi said excitedly. "But you said he's not expecting a child anytime soon, so that means it's something else."

"Are he and Suzan that serious?" Myra asked.

"Yeah, like Orson said, they've been together for less than six months," Naomi added.

"I wonder why he wants to meet with me," Ruby said. She stared at Maggie for a moment, then her eyes grew wide. "Unless he's going to ask me about using my barn sometime in the near future."

"That's it," Myra shrieked, clapping her hands together. "He's going to ask you to use the barn."

"Would you women please calm down?" Orson shouted over them. "If someone walked into the dining room right now and heard you back here hollering, they'd call the police."

"Let them. Some good it would do." Maggie laughed.

The kitchen grew quiet. Ruby wiped a tear from her eye. "Does Bradley want to talk to me about the use of my barn?"

Maggie bit the inside of her lip as long as she could stand it. She wanted desperately to tell them, but she knew it wasn't her place to say a word. Her son Bradley, single father and proprietor of the second donut shop location Hunter Springs, had indeed found someone he loved and was serious about. She knew the use of the barn had nothing to do with the wedding but everything to do with a special location to ask his significant other an important question.

"Okay, okay! Fine," Maggie shouted suddenly. "Bradley and Suzan may have only been together for a short time, but if you all remember, they met a year ago when they attended a petting zoo field trip the daycare hosted. As you all know, she has a little girl herself, and they're the cutest little family. He wants to use the barn so he can pop the question." She held her stomach, gasping for air.

"Wow," Ruby said, walking toward the baker's

table. "I can't believe you didn't tell me this sooner." She placed her hands softly on Maggie's arm.

"I was trying to respect his privacy, but I just couldn't hold it in any longer," Maggie admitted. "Brett took him ring shopping last weekend. Bradley already has the whole thing planned out."

The room erupted in cheers and hugs. Even Orson, still perched on his wooden stool, smiled broadly and held out his arms to Maggie offering a congratulatory embrace. They chatted for several minutes about Bradley, Suzan, and Suzan's little girl, Chloe.

After the tears were shed and the hugs repeated, Orson stood up and pulled his wallet out of his pants. He slipped out a twenty-dollar bill and handed it over to Maggie. "Here," he said quietly. "Put this toward the bed, and if you find something for the little girl, use that, too."

"It's okay," Maggie said. "Brett and I can buy Wyatt his bed." She pushed the money back toward him.

Ruby cleared her throat. "I don't think it's about whether you can afford it or not," she said softly. "It's about a grandpa taking care of his family."

CHAPTER TWO

Maggie worked hard through the lunch rush. She pulled the empty trays out of the display case and washed the dishes before signaling to Naomi that she was ready to head out.

"We've got it from here," Ruby said when Maggie checked in with her. "If I need any help, I'll draft Orson to wash dishes or wait on customers."

Orson raised his hand from the Old Timer's Table. "I can take orders," he said without looking up from the newspaper.

"Ready?" Naomi asked when she tossed her soiled apron into the hamper just inside the storage room.

"Let's go," Maggie said. She opened the back

door and followed Naomi to her small truck. "How many sales do you plan to hit this afternoon?"

"Well, we can start by checking out the furniture first, then go up the road toward the lake," Naomi suggested.

"I was hoping you'd say that. I want to get there before the bed sells."

Naomi pulled the car down the alley and turned left. They drove toward the center of town and into a newer subdivision. Maggie watched for the address and signaled when they reached the two-story brick house.

"I think this is it," she said.

"It sure looks like it." Naomi parked in front of the curb near the mailbox and minutes later, each woman carried one end of a solid wood toddler bed to the truck. They went back for the matching dresser that the seller had thrown in with it.

"I guess Myra caught a break today, too," Maggie said when they returned to the cab of the truck.

"You're not going to keep it with the bed?"

Maggie shook her head. "I had explicit orders from my son not to add anything more to it. Where do you want to go next?"

"There's a large yard sale about three streets

over," Naomi said. "It's supposed to be a very popular sale."

"Where'd you hear that?" Maggie asked.

"Online," Naomi said as she drove. "I'm part of a yard sale group."

"I'm embarrassed to admit that I have no idea what that means."

Naomi shrugged as she steered her truck around the block. "You know, just a page on social media for yard sale enthusiasts. We all live around the Ozarks, and we chat about the best sales. Some people take this stuff pretty seriously, you know."

"It sure sounds that way," Maggie said. As much as she didn't want to sound like Orson, she had a difficult time understanding why someone would put that much time into it.

Naomi laughed "There are always a handful of people, older women usually, who are in search of some knick-knack or a collector's item or another."

"What do they do, trade shopping tips?"

"Oh, no. It's far more serious than that," Naomi said. "They act like they're hunting for ancient arti- facts or dinosaur bones or something. They discuss places where these items might have been spotted and they track down items in antique stores and go into full on Jessica Fletcher mode with the antique shop owners, trying to figure out where they might have found a particular piece or something."

"It sounds like they're more antique shoppers than yard sale enthusiasts."

"Yard Sailors," Naomi said.

"Pardon me?"

"Yard Sailors," Naomi said again. "That's what they call themselves."

"Oh," Maggie said. "That's umm... That's a clever name, I suppose."

"Anyway, they go into the antique shops to find out where a certain item came from, and then they do an entire investigation on it. As soon as they have a location, they start hitting yard sales in those areas to see if some ignorant civilian might have slapped a fifty-cent sticker on a priceless item. Sometimes they get very lucky."

"How lucky?" Maggie asked.

"You ever watch that TV show where some old man finds out his grandma's vase is worth twenty-grand?"

"Yeah, a time or two," Maggie said.

"That lucky."

"Wow." Maggie gave a low whistle. "No wonder they call other people things like 'ignorant civilians.'"

"They do get pretty caught up in all of it," Naomi said.

"So, what are you looking for today?"

"Nothing quite that serious," Naomi said. "I'm trying to find a few missing pieces to a canister set I found last year. Nothing too valuable, just sentimental, I guess."

"Do you have a picture?" Maggie asked. "I can help you look."

"I have a description, but I have to warn you. This sale in particular was very popular in the online group. We're bound to see a lot of people there."

"As long as nobody gets in my way, we'll be fine." Maggie clutched her purse in her lap and leaned forward in her seat. Naomi giggled and beat the steering wheel as she drove.

The popularity of the sale was evident as soon as Naomi pulled onto the road. Cars lined the entire street, and Naomi was forced to drive around the block twice before a space opened up. When she parked at last, Maggie was shocked at the expanse of the sale. Items were spread over three separate lawns. The sale even extended into the back yard at two of the houses.

"This is huge," Maggie said.

"And very popular," Naomi said as they waited

for the third car to pass before they could make it across the street. She pointed to several tables set up in the front yard of the center house. Each table was filled with a figurine or statuette, with several grouped in small collections.

Maggie noticed a group of a dozen elderly women eyeing each piece.

"They're like hunters going after a big game trophy," Naomi leaned over and whispered to Maggie. "I'd stay out of their way if I were you."

"Do you want to split up and look for your canister set?" Maggie asked. "I just need to know what I'm looking for."

"Don't laugh at me," Naomi said, blushing slightly. "But they're shaped like mushrooms. The top is the cap of the mushroom, and the bottom is the stem."

"Oh, I think I know the canisters you're talking about," Maggie said. An image burst into her head. She could see the old canisters lining the counter of her great-aunt Marjorie's house on the hill outside of town. The place was now a bed and breakfast run by her good friend, Gretchen LeClair.

"Great," Naomi said. "I'll start over here on the right."

"I'll go left, and we can meet back here in the

middle." She headed toward the back yard of the first house on the left, and walked past a large group of people going over several stacks of clothing that were piled on the ground. She shivered, thinking of the various chiggers and mites that must be climbing through the layers of fabric.

She was surprised to see several pieces of play equipment for smaller children. Maggie took her time inspecting a slide and a playhouse. She intended to find Naomi and ask whether or not she could make room in the back of her small pickup truck for the slide. It would be a mutual gift for both of the children.

Maggie walked back around the front of the first house and headed to the front yard of the one in the middle. She heard raised voices and spotted several women gathered around a square card table. Four women were gathered on one side. A couple of them raised their fingers as they spoke animatedly to the lone woman on the opposite side of the table.

As she walked closer, Maggie expected to see a table filled with valuable items. Not sure what she would find, she was dumbfounded to see one of the women holding onto a small figurine of an old woman with a pointy chin riding on the back of a winged bird. The woman had the figurine in a death grip. More figurines filled the center of the table, but the other women ignored them, focusing only on the Mother Goose figurine.

"I want that," one of the four women demanded. Her white hair was cropped close to her head.

"You can't have it," the woman across the table said. "I saw it first."

"Give it to me or you will regret it," the short-haired woman said.

"You tell her, Doris," one of her companions said. Unlike Doris, her hair hung in wild wisps around her head. The rest was pinned up in a high bun.

"I found it first. Fair and square," the woman holding the figurine said. "Just go on and leave me alone. I aim to go pay for this and get out of here."

"You aren't going anywhere with that," another one of the women said.

"I'll handle this, Linda," Doris said to her companion. She focused on the first woman. "Look here, whatever your name is. We were already interested in that piece when you came along and swooped it up. Linda and I are collectors, and Olivia and Kim are experts on them. We drove all the way down here from Indiana, and you have to let go."

"I don't have to let go of a thing," the woman said. Linda moved a step closer to the corner of the table. The first woman clutched the figurine to her chest and took a step backward. "I'm getting out of here now."

"Not so fast," one of the other women said. Maggie wasn't sure if it was Olivia or Kim.

"This is getting really scary," Naomi said in her ear. Maggie jumped; unaware anyone had come up behind her.

"Why are they so crazy about that figurine?" Maggie whispered. "It looks like that one lady had it first."

"That's Janine," Naomi said. "She was asking the owner of this house about it and those other women overheard her. They followed her to the table and circled her like a ring of sharks when she picked it up. I don't think she's walking out of here with it."

Maggie gasped. "Do you think they would try to physically take it from her?"

"I'm not sure, but just look at them. They aren't taking no for an answer."

Naomi was right. The four women had left their station on the far side of the table and began slowly walking toward Janine. Maggie found herself gripping Naomi's arm as the suspenseful scene unfolded. She had no idea why she was so intrigued by the ridiculous display, but she couldn't take her eyes off them.

"Do we have an issue here?" A young blonde woman stalked across the green grass toward them. "If there's a problem, I'm going to have to ask all of you to leave."

"There's no issue," Janine said, holding up the statute. "I found this first, and then these ladies tried to crowd around me. I was just coming to you to purchase it. Can we take care of that now?"

"No. The four of us were already looking at it when she came along and got it," Doris argued.

"Yeah, it's rightfully ours," Linda said. She walked around the table and stood just inches from Janine.

"I don't care who had it first," the young woman said. "This lady has it now, and she's the one who gets to leave here with it. The rest of you go find something else to look at or you need to move along to a different sale."

"I don't think you understand," Doris said, stopping the woman. "We are part of a group that's been hunting these collectibles for over twenty years. You need to let us purchase it."

"Look, we'd be more than happy to buy you anything else you want at this sale," one of the other women, either Olivia or Kim, stepped forward to say. "I don't care what it is. You pick it out, and we'll buy it. Just let us have the figurine."

The homeowner sighed and shook her finger at the women. "I have no idea why that little thing is so important to the four of you, but I've already said what's going to happen. This lady here gets to buy it. I think it's time for the four of you to move along."

"We'll move along as soon as she hands that over and you let us pay you for it," Linda said. She placed her hand on Janine's wrist.

"That's just not going to happen," Janine said, shaking her arm free. She stumbled backward for a moment, then gulped in a deep breath of air and clutched her chest. A second later, Janine was on her knees. Mother Goose fell from her grip and landed on the ground. She followed soon after, landing face first on the soft grass.

For a moment, no one moved a muscle. They simply stared at the older woman. Maggie shook herself into reality and shouted to anyone who would listen. "Someone, call an ambulance," she said. Her own phone was back in Naomi's truck. "Please! We need help here."

Several other yard sale shoppers came rushing over. One of them, a good-looking man in his mid-thirties, landed on his knees next to Janine. He expertly picked up her wrist and began searching for a pulse. "I can't get anything." He dropped her hand and reached under her neck, hesitating for a moment as if listening for something. A moment later, he sat back up, resting his palms on his thighs and dropping his head. "I'm afraid it's too late."

"That is so unfortunate," Doris said. She edged closer to Janine. Bending down, she quietly reached for the figurine and pushed it behind her feet. "Are you sure we shouldn't still call for an ambulance?"

"What are you doing, lady?" the homeowner shouted.

"I have no idea what you're talking about," Doris said.

"I saw you," the young woman said. "I saw you push that figurine behind your feet. A woman is dead, and you're worried about that? I think it's time for you to get off my property. Now."

"I think you're overreacting just a bit," Linda said. "Besides, you're holding a yard sale here. It's not like the police are going to come and make us leave and everyone else gets to stay."

"You're wrong," the young woman said. She raised her head and looked around. "Everyone, listen up. The yard sale is over. Drop what you have in your hands and leave this property at once."

"You don't want to do that," Linda warned.

"I just did it," the woman said. "If you're not off my property in thirty seconds, I'm calling the police."

CHAPTER THREE

"That was insane," Naomi said when they returned to the donut shop. She parked her truck behind Maggie's car. "I can't believe we just saw that lady die."

"Neither can I," Maggie said. Her mind was still on the scene that unfolded in front of them. The four women refused to leave, even when the ambulance arrived. Brooks Macklin, Myra's husband and Dogwood Mountain Police Chief, had to intervene when Doris refused to let go of the Mother Goose figurine. She held on for dear life as long as she could. Finally, Brett and a few deputies arrived at the scene and escorted the women off the property.

"I think it was her heart. At least, that's what the paramedics had to say."

"You heard them talking?" Maggie asked. A

feeling bubbled up in her middle, but she was unsure what she was feeling.

"I wasn't trying to listen, but I was curious, so I didn't ignore it, either."

"If she did, it's probably because of the stress those other women put on her," Maggie said. She shivered at the thought. "They were like vultures surrounding her."

"At least they didn't get their way in the end." Naomi waited while Maggie got out of the truck before giving her a wave and pulling back out of the alley behind the donut shop.

Maggie decided to head inside the kitchen for a few moments. Brett wasn't due home for a couple of hours, and she felt the need for something sweet. She flipped on the lights and went straight for the cooler where she hoped Ruby had saved a few of the day's leftover donuts. She craved something chocolate and fluffy, but it was clear they had sold out of everything.

"Well, shoot," Maggie said. She stood in the middle of the cooler for a moment, then walked out and shut the door behind her.

A small batch of donuts wouldn't take long. Months had passed since she last stood in the middle of the donut shop kitchen in the mood to create. She headed to the storage room to gather the fixings for a basic yeast-raised donut. She loaded her arms with flour, yeast, sugar, and salt. Once the dough was rising, Maggie returned to the storage room for more ingredients.

She collected several toppings, including hot fudge, chocolate icing, coconut, maraschino cherries, and canisters of crushed candies and cookies. When the dough was ready, she cut out two dozen donuts and set them in the warmer to proof along with the donut holes. As soon as the dough was risen and ready, Maggie placed the donuts in the deep fryer and waited until the batch was golden brown.

After a few minutes of cooling, Maggie gazed at the array of ingredients in front of her. She picked up the chocolate icing and warmed it in the microwave for a few moments, then returned to the baker's table. She glazed the yeast donuts with chocolate icing first. As soon as the glaze was set, she stirred a small container of fudge and frosted a few donuts holes. She popped one in her mouth and smiled, then spread the fudge over the remaining donuts.

Next, she added sweetened coconut, chopped cherries, bits of crushed pretzels, and chopped nuts. To finish off her masterpiece, she drizzled caramel sauce over the top and stepped back. She returned the ingredients to the storage room while the donuts set for a few more minutes.

As she was waiting, she heard a key turn in the back door lock. Ruby stepped inside and stared at the new creations on the table. "What's all this?" she asked.

"Have one," Maggie said, gesturing toward the baker's table. "I just threw the kitchen sink at it."

"Looks like you didn't leave much out," Ruby joked. She picked up a donut and took a bite. "Whoa. These are delicious."

"Thanks." Maggie beamed.

"Kitchen Sink Donuts."

"I like that. Do you think they're good enough to put in the display case?"

"Absolutely," Ruby said around a second bite. "I have a feeling these are going to be an instant hit."

"I guess so," Maggie said, amazed at the gusto her best friend finished the donut off with.

"You better box the rest of these up and take them home to your husband," Ruby suggested. "Because they're not going to last long around here."

"I have a feeling he's not going to be home for a little while anyway," Maggie said.

"Why, was there a riot at the local yard sale?" Ruby rolled her eyes.

"Just about," Maggie said.

"Wait, what? I was just kidding," Ruby said. "What happened?"

"Well, for one thing, a woman named Janine dropped dead." Maggie shook her head. "Naomi overheard the paramedics attending to her say it had something to do with her heart, but I feel like there's more to it than that."

"Hold on a minute," Ruby said. "You watched a woman have a heart attack or something, and now you doubt that's what happened? Fill me in. I think I'm missing something here because it sounds to me like you're actually looking for a murder to solve."

"We went to a large yard sale Naomi was very excited about," Maggie began. "There were three houses in a row that hosted it. The middle house, where all this took place, had a lot of those knick-knacks and figurines I remember seeing in my great-aunt's house. Anyway, a group of ladies practically surrounded the woman. She had this Mother Goose figurine, and they wanted it, bad. They acted like a bunch of sharks circling their prey."

"Did they attack her or something?" Ruby asked. "I'm still not understanding why you doubt what she passed away from."

"When I tell you they circled like sharks, I'm not

kidding," Maggie continued. "They pushed her and pushed her and then suddenly, the homeowner came out and threatened to have them all escorted off the property. That's when Janine dropped to her knees and keeled over."

"It sounds like a classic heart attack to me," Ruby said.

"As soon as she went down, the ringleader of the sharks, Doris, came over and tried to sneak away with the figurine," Maggie said with a shudder. "I've never seen anything like it. Who cares that much about a dusty old knick knack?"

"It sounds like those women did," Ruby said. "Even so, I'm sure it was an unfortunate chain of events, but it was warm outside today. If this Janine woman got overheated and had a bad heart in the first place, it's very likely she died from a heart attack. The added stress wouldn't have helped."

Maggie folded her arms and rested on Orson's stool. She shook her head and raised her eyes at Ruby. "Something tells me there's more to the story than that."

"Are you planning to look further into this?"

"I'm not sure, but I really want to know why that stupid figurine mattered enough to them that they'd harass a woman to death over it."

CHAPTER FOUR

"The coroner listed her death as natural causes," Brett told her a few minutes after he arrived home from work. Maggie directed him to the platter of Kitchen Sink Donuts on the table. "Oh, these look divine." He picked up a donut hole and popped it into his mouth.

"Are you sure?" Maggie asked. "The way those women circled around her gives me the chills."

"Her heart stopped," Brett said, his mouth still full. "Janine Lawrence was a seventy-eight-year-old woman with a very bad heart. Her doctor had warned her about being in the heat too long, according to her daughter."

"Sweetheart, you didn't see those women." Maggie took a seat at the table. "All four of them looked like they would take a bite out of her for that figurine, but what I don't understand is why? What is so remarkable about an old Mother Goose figurine?"

"There's nothing to look into here."

"Are you sure? I mean, how many times have you heard of someone dying at a yard sale?"

"I'm not sure I like where this conversation is going," Brett said. "You really need to leave this alone."

"Why? Is there something else you know?" Maggie pressed, narrowing her eyes at him.

"Sweetheart, listen to yourself," Brett said, suddenly exasperated. He threw his hands up in the air. "You're reading too much into what I'm saying. All I know is that an unfortunate event happened at a yard sale in town today. An old woman died and now her daughter is on her way here to deal with her arrangements. That's it. There's nothing more to the story."

"Oh, my goodness," Maggie said. "Did that really happen?"

"Huh?" Brett raised a brow.

"Did we actually just have our very first Lucy and Ricky moment?"

He stared blankly at her. "What do Lucy and Ricky have to do with anything?"

"You just gave me the husband warning," Maggie

said. "'Now Lucy, you are not going to be in the show, and you know it. Stay home and behave yourself like a good wife.'"

"Is that what I sound like?" Brett said.

"A little, but without the accent." Maggie laughed. "It sounded like you were telling me to back off from asking questions about this."

"I didn't mean to just sound that way," Brett said. "That's actually what I'm saying. There's nothing more to this than what happened."

Maggie reached for another donut hole. "We really shouldn't be eating these for dinner," she said, taking a bite. "Is there anything wrong with me asking questions?"

"Of course not, as long as those questions don't turn into harassing a group of people about a crime that was never committed."

"Wow, that was harsh." Maggie frowned.

"I just meant those four women didn't do anything wrong, as far as I could tell. Remember, I was there afterward, too."

"I'm at least going to look into that figurine," Maggie said. "If nothing more than for my own understanding. I have to know why they cared so much about it."

"I don't see any harm in that," Brett said. "Just

tread lightly with the people involved, okay? I don't want the victim's daughter to report you for harassing her for information."

"Do you actually think I would do something like that?" Maggie asked, a little astonished. "After all, I was there. I watched her mother take her last breath."

"No. I'm sorry. Of course, I don't think that."

"It sure sounds like you do." Maggie stood up and pushed her chair under the table.

"Where are you going?" Brett asked when she headed for the back door.

"I suddenly feel like taking a walk," Maggie said. She tried to hold in her anger and frustration, but it was evident on her face.

"Honey, I said I was sorry," Brett said. "I don't want to fight about this."

"Then don't, but I am still going for a walk. I feel like seeing the Dogwood House right now."

"You're going to walk that far?" Brett asked. "What about dinner?"

"Surprise me," Maggie said, shutting the door behind her. She stood outside for a moment, considering rushing back inside into Brett's arms. The last thing she wanted to do was fight with him. They hadn't been married long enough to accumulate that many big fights and she didn't want to start now.

Maybe she was wrong. Maybe it was simple, but something told her to look further. She had been wrong before, there was no doubt about that, but she had also been right, a few times. She had learned to trust her instincts, and they were screaming at her that the four women at the yard sale were up to no good.

Maggie walked several blocks before she reached the road that led up the hill past her Aunt Marjorie 's old house. The Dogwood House, like the one she occupied with Brett, had once belonged to her great-aunt, Marjorie Getz. Following her death, Maggie inherited both the donut shop and the small cottage in town. The larger house was sold a couple of times before it wound up in the hands of Gretchen LeClair, Maggie's friend and Orson's companion. Gretchen had turned it into a bed and breakfast. Despite the daily morning deliveries of coffee and pastries for the guests, Maggie hadn't been to the property in some time.

"Hello," Albert, Gretchen's handyman and groundskeeper, called out when she headed up the road.

"Hey, there," Maggie said. She stopped for a moment out of politeness, but a conversation was not what she was looking for.

"Oh," Gretchen said, walking down the driveway.

"You're out awfully late for a walk. Would you like to come inside?"

"That's not necessary, but thank you."

"Nonsense," Gretchen said. "I insist you come inside for a moment. We can share a cup of tea and you can take a rest before you head back home." She turned and headed back toward the rear of the house. Maggie felt compelled to follow.

"It is a little late for a walk," Maggie acknowledged when she took a seat at the small kitchen table. Despite the updated decorating, the place still felt like her aunt's large kitchen, and she was a small child seated at the table.

"Sometimes our souls just need a breather," Gretchen said. She switched on the electric kettle and waited for the water to boil. "What do you fancy? Chamomile? Ginger tea?"

"I'm up for anything, thank you," Maggie said. She folded her hands on the table in front of her.

"All right, chamomile it is," Gretchen said, placing a tea bag in a mug for her. She poured hot water over the tea bag and set the mug in front of Maggie at the table. "Now, suppose you tell me what's on your mind."

"Thank you," Maggie said. "There isn't much on my mind tonight."

"More nonsense," Gretchen declared. "I've known you long enough to notice that your thoughts are twisted up in your head tonight, which is the reason I suspect you took a walk in the first place. Now spill it."

"It's really nothing," Maggie said. She blew on the hot tea before she took a sip. "I had a few words with Brett about something I witnessed at a yard sale today."

"Oh, goodness," Gretchen said. "Don't tell me you were there when that poor old lady passed away."

"You heard about that?" Maggie asked.

"Naturally," Gretchen said. "I don't have to tell you how the rumor mill runs in this town. It was all over the neighborhood page this afternoon."

"You mean online?"

"Well, yes," Gretchen said. "I'm on social media, after all. The news about that poor woman's death was as well. Do you know what happened? There are a lot of rumors going around."

"Like what exactly?" Maggie asked, her eyes widening. "But to answer your question, yes, I was there. I watched it all happen."

"So, what do you think?" Gretchen asked, leaning in slightly. "Did that woman die of heart problems? Or was foul played involved?"

"That is exactly what Brett and I just argued over," Maggie said.

"Seriously?"

Maggie nodded her head vigorously. "I have a feeling there's something more to it, but he says the coroner ruled it natural causes. He warned me not to get involved."

"Do you think he's right?"

"He's right about not prying so much that I bother the woman's daughter, but I would never do that. I just want to follow up on this feeling that's nagging me."

"Then you should do it," Gretchen said. "Your instincts are never wrong. I've seen that in the time we've known each other. If your gut instinct tells you to look into this, that's what you should do."

Maggie shook her head. "I've never seen people act so crazy over a simple figurine," she said. "You should have seen those women."

"Well, depending on the figurine, I believe it," Gretchen said. "Most of the public has no idea how fierce the competition for certain antique pieces can be."

"You're not the first person I've heard that from," Maggie said.

"A lot of people wouldn't believe it, but there's a

black market for that stuff. Some figurines are so lucrative people will commit armed robbery to get their hands on them. What sort of piece was it?"

"It was just a Mother Goose piece," Maggie said. "It couldn't have been more than six inches tall, but those women were determined."

"Mother Goose statues can fetch a pretty penny," Gretchen said. "You should go talk to an antiques dealer and ask them how fierce collectors can be about that stuff. I've even heard of people going to jail because they were so determined to get their hands on just the right item. Individually, they can bring in thousands of dollars, but as a complete collection, that's where the big money is."

"It's not that I don't believe it; I just don't see the value in those old things."

"I'm right there with you," Gretchen said. "The thing is, they're not asking us. It's what the market demands that determines how far people will go to cash in."

Darkness was just beginning to settle when Maggie walked back home. She was surprised to see Brett's pickup truck slowing down when she was halfway there. He rolled down the window and smiled. "You were gone a long time," he said. "I was beginning to worry about you."

"I had tea with Gretchen," Maggie said.

"Why don't you get in and we'll go home together?"

She nodded and walked around the side of the pickup. "We had an interesting discussion. Apparently, those Mother Goose figurines are quite lucrative. The behavior I saw with those other women is not that shocking after all."

"That's interesting," Brett said, not looking her way. "But I have more interesting news."

"What's that?" Maggie asked, a little irritated by his lack of interest in what she had to say.

"The secretary from the county coroner's office called me about five minutes ago. It turns out, the coroner has rescinded her finding of natural causes. She's determined the death of Janine Lawrence to be inconclusive."

"Inconclusive?" Maggie asked. "What changed?"

"I don't know what prompted her to do it, but she took a closer look. She determined that Janine did not die from a heart attack. She died of heart failure, but the actual cause wasn't immediately evident."

"So, what happens now?"

"Now we wait for more information, but I wouldn't be surprised if Brooks doesn't open an investigation into her death."

"Then my suspicions were not so misplaced after all," Maggie said.

"Now, listen here, Lucy," Brett said in his best Ricky voice.

Maggie laughed. "Seriously, though. Gretchen was saying competition for these figurines can get pretty fierce. There's even a black market."

"Hold on a minute," Brett said. "We need to be careful pointing fingers at people who may have had nothing to do with the woman's death. Do you know what I'm saying?"

"I know exactly what you're saying." Maggie turned and gazed out the window as they drove the rest of the way home. Her thoughts were all over the place.

CHAPTER FIVE

"Did you hear anything from Brett about that lady's death yesterday?" Naomi asked as soon as she walked into the kitchen the next morning.

Maggie stood over the baker's table, putting the finishing touches on the first batch of Kitchen Sink Donuts. "We talked a little bit about it, yeah," she said, not looking up.

"What did he say?" Naomi asked.

Maggie forced herself to smile. "Just that the coroner changed the cause of death from natural causes to inconclusive."

"The cause of death was changed?" Ruby asked, suddenly interested. "That's not very common."

"This is a tough one because Janine, the woman who died, did have heart problems," Maggie said.

"But after looking into things a little further, it was clear that's not how she died."

"How can they tell that?" Naomi asked. She hung her purse on a hook and removed an apron, tying it around her waist.

"I honestly have no idea, but Brett reminded me that still doesn't mean the woman was murdered."

"Do you really think the woman at the yard sale might have been murdered?" Myra asked.

"That's not what I meant," Maggie said, quickly reversing. "I've just had a feeling that something about the whole situation was off."

"I'd have to agree," Naomi said. "It's odd how they were all circling her, and then she suddenly dropped dead. Those four other women were very interested in what she was about to purchase."

"Like sharks in the water," Maggie said. "According to Gretchen, that isn't entirely unheard of for some of those figurines, either. I walked up there last night, and we had tea together. She told me there's a lot of drama involved."

"Yeah, but there's a difference between drama and cold-blooded murder," Myra said. "You'd think to pull off something like that in broad daylight, you'd have to be a fairly sophisticated killer."

"You've been married to Brooks way too long,"

Orson grumbled as he walked the rest of the way in through the swinging door and took his seat on his stool. "You sound like a true crime documentary or something."

"Thanks," Myra said. "You always know how to make a girl feel good."

"You know I'm just picking on you," Orson said. "It's your fault for buying that cheap toilet paper." He grinned. Brooks and Myra had purchased and renovated an old home that included a separate apartment for Orson who had become like a father to Myra. He was always giving them a hard time about something.

"Anyway, back to this case," Myra said.

"See what I mean? Sounds like cop talk to me." He shook his head.

"I'm curious," Ruby cut in. "What else did Gretchen say about those figurines? Exactly how much money are we talking about?"

"That's the thing that really got me," Maggie said. "By themselves, some old figurines demand a few thousand dollars, but she said that when they're included in an entire collection, it just goes up from there. There's even a black market for the things."

"You know what that means," Orson said.

"I have no idea," Maggie said, somewhat impatiently. Orson had a habit of interrupting when things were just getting good. "What does that mean?"

"Black market means people are willing to pay just about anything to get their hands on it," Orson said. "A black market also means stolen goods."

"Are you saying people would be willing to commit a crime to get one of those figurines?" Naomi asked.

"That's exactly right," Orson said. "I don't care what the item is, if there's a black market for it, there's someone willing to break the law to get it and get paid for it."

"I hadn't thought of that," Maggie said.

"What are you going to do?" Ruby asked. "Because I know you're not going to let this go."

"After work, I'm going to Hunter Springs," Maggie announced, thinking out loud. "There's an antique store there I want to check out. I'm going to ask a few questions about the figurines."

"And what will that tell you?" Myra asked.

"It might tell me whether or not the figurine those ladies were fighting over was worth anything," Maggie said.

"What will that prove?" Myra asked.

"I'm not sure yet," Maggie said. "But it feels like

the direction I should take. Do you have an objection to me going?"

"Oh, not at all," Myra said, smiling. "I'm just curious. There doesn't seem to be a lot of information about things right now. but if you have a gut instinct, I think you should follow it."

When the conversation lulled, Maggie returned her attention to her work, but her thoughts drifted back to the figurines.

"Can someone please explain what's going on out there in the display case?" Orson asked a little while later.

"What's wrong?" Ruby asked.

"Those donuts," Orson said. "The ones Maggie worked on earlier. What are they?"

"It's just something I put together yesterday when I had a craving after the yard sale," Maggie said. "Ruby called them Kitchen Sink Donuts because they include a little bit of everything."

"Well, you might need to make a few more," Orson said sheepishly.

"Why?" Maggie asked. "We haven't even opened the doors yet."

"Even so, you might want to add a few more to the display case," Orson said, then quickly reversed back through the swinging door into the dining room.

"You better follow him and find out what happened," Myra suggested.

Maggie tossed her towel on the baker's table. She wiped the cinnamon off her hands onto her apron and followed Orson through the door. He was seated at his usual spot and smiled in her direction. Maggie headed over to the display case and stared. "Orson, would you care to explain why there are six donuts missing from the tray I just put out here?"

"No, thank you," Orson called across the dining room.

"What do you mean, no thank you?" Maggie said. She planted both hands on her hips. "Did you take the donuts or not?"

"That's not the question you asked me," Orson said. "You just asked me if I cared to explain, and I don't."

"What happened?" Myra asked, joining Maggie behind the display case.

"That happened," Maggie said, pointing to the empty spots on the tray. "Apparently, someone helped himself to a half dozen donuts."

"Orson, do you have anything to say about this?" Myra asked.

"Nope," Orson said. "Sure don't."

"He is impossible," Maggie said, sighing heavily.

"He may be impossible," Orson called out. "But he sure isn't hungry."

Myra grabbed Maggie by her hand and pulled her back into the kitchen. They made it to the storage room before both women broke out in the giggles. "All I have to say is try living with the old man," Myra said, shaking her head.

After several hours of working, Maggie announced that she was heading out. Myra and Naomi had the run of the place for the rest of the day. Ruby had taken off early to meet the veterinarian on her farm to look after some goats, and Maggie was headed to Hunter Springs. She planned to stop in and see Bradley at the donut shop before checking out the antique store.

"Hey, Mom," Bradley said when he called her five minutes after she left work. "Is there any way we can change our plans to tomorrow?"

"Of course," Maggie said. "Is anything wrong?"

"No, everything is fine," Bradley said. "I just had a change in plans. Suzan got off work early and we're going to run up to Joplin for a nice dinner."

"Are you taking the kids?" Maggie asked.

"No, we're not taking the kids," Bradley said. His tone was odd. "Suzan's younger sister is babysitting."

"Bradley is tonight going to be a special night?"

Maggie asked. "Are you going to ask Suzan a certain question?"

"Yeah, I think I am." He was breathless. "I know I planned other things, but I just feel like tonight is the right time."

"I'm so happy for you," Maggie said. She blinked quickly to remove the tears from her eyes. "I want to hear all about it."

"You will," Bradley said.

After the phone call ended, Maggie headed for the antique store. She parked in front of the three-story Victorian style house. Several pieces lined the covered front porch, and when she stepped inside, she was surprised by the electronic sounding doorbell that alerted the owners to her arrival.

"Good afternoon." A tall woman emerged from a door to her right. She stood behind a small counter with the register at the front. She was poised and proper, much like Maggie would have pictured a Victorian woman to look. "Are you here looking for something specific?"

"I am, actually," Maggie said. "I'm interested in figurines. Specifically, a Mother Goose figurine. Do you carry those?"

"You do realize that's like asking a liquor store if they carry beer," the woman said, scoffing slightly.

Maggie was immediately taken aback by her crass tone. "Are you just looking for a figurine in general? Or do you have any more information you would like to share with me about this figurine."

"Okay, obviously I'm not a collector, but I do have some questions. Do you have time to answer them?"

"Sure," the woman said, smiling broadly. "After all, what would I have to do with the rest of my day other than answering your questions about a figurine." She drew out the last part of the word figurine, emphasizing her disdain for the question.

"Alright, then," Maggie said, determined to be pleasant despite the woman's manner. "How hard is it to find complete collections of the figurines?"

"Again, that is a wildly broad question you're asking."

"I'm so sorry," she said. "I didn't catch your name. I'm Maggie, by the way."

"Well, Maggie," the woman said. "My name is Opal. Opal Olbermann. I am the proprietor of this antique store."

"Alright then, Opal," Maggie said brightly. "I honestly have no idea about valuable figurines, but I was at a yard sale yesterday and I watched four women almost attack another woman who held one of them in her hand. Unfortunately, the woman passed away right then and there. I guess I'm a little confused why one of those statues would matter so much to someone."

"The woman died?" Opal asked. She dropped her shoulders and folded her light arms over her narrow chest.

"Yes," Maggie said. "I know it sounds silly, but something about her death just doesn't seem right."

"Of course not, dear," Opal said. "Who wants to die at a yard sale?"

"I guess I'm just wondering what could be so special about them," Maggie said. "The woman's last experience was four women coming after her like vultures for a figurine."

"I'm sure you've already heard that some of those figurines can command a great deal of money," Opal said. "Otherwise, why would you visit an antique store?"

"I spoke with my friend over at the Dogwood House in Dogwood Mountain," Maggie admitted. "And Gretchen told me that anything related to Mother Goose can be valuable."

"I know Gretchen LeClair well," Opal said. "And it isn't just Mother Goose that commands high value. You must understand that some of those figurines go back to the early days of our country. Mother Goose alone has been around for centuries. People have been making figurines and statues of Mother Goose and those characters for hundreds of years. Some of them are very valuable. Can you describe this particular figurine?"

"It was around six inches tall. It depicted a woman with a pointy chin riding on the back of a goose," Maggie said. "Beyond that, I don't remember much."

"Do you remember if the goose was wearing anything?" Opal said.

"The goose? I think it had a blue hat on its head." Maggie shrugged. She strained to picture the figurine. "I only got a quick look at it."

"Well, if the goose was wearing a hat and an apron it is likely that it is part of a collection dating back to the Revolutionary War," Opal said. Her tone changed and she smiled as she spoke. "I'm not sure how much Gretchen told you, but an antique Staffordshire figurine of Mother Goose was sold along with a statue of Little Bo Peep at an auction in London five years ago for half a million dollars."

"That's incredible," Maggie said. "How do people find them? I can't imagine all four of those women just happened to be at that yard sale and recognized the statue as something antique and valuable."

"People get pretty serious about it," Opal said. "I keep the figurines we sell under lock and key for that reason."

"Do you think that statue was, what did you call it, an antique Staffordshire figurine?"

"Not with the hat and the apron," Opal said.

"Has anyone been in here looking for that type of figurine recently?" Maggie asked.

"Aside from you, no," Opal said. The stiffness in her shoulders returned. "Now, dear, if you don't mind, I do have quite a bit of work to do. I hope I've answered your questions thoroughly."

"Thank you for your time," Maggie said, heading for the door. Her shoulders sagged in disappointment. What had she hoped to learn by coming here? She knew a little more than she had when she left the Dogwood House, but not much. It was clearer now than ever that small figurines could be highly valued, but she hadn't learned much more than that.

CHAPTER SIX

Maggie sat in the front seat of her car for a moment. She gripped the steering wheel and shook her head. There was no way to tell if Janine's death had been deliberate or not. In truth, she hadn't seen any of the women lay their hands on her.

She planned to head straight home, frustrated with herself and just about everything else that was happening. Perhaps more time in the kitchen would help clear her mind. The Kitchen Sink Donut had been selling well, so creating another new donut might be just what she needed to make herself feel better.

A car honked behind her, breaking Maggie from her thoughts where she sat at the stop sign just down the road. She jumped in her seat and waved in the mirror, signaling an apology. When she caught a glimpse of the driver, she felt her muscles tighten.

"Doris," she said to herself. When the woman honked again, Maggie made a fast decision and turned on her hazard lights. She rolled down the window and stepped out of her car.

The woman rolled down her window as Maggie stepped up to it. "Is there something wrong?"

"I'm so sorry," she said, clutching her hand over her heart. "I think there's something wrong with my car. You might have to go around me."

"What's the matter with your car?" Doris asked.

"I don't know." Maggie looked over and gazed toward her car. "It smells funny. A weird smell is coming out through the vents."

"But it otherwise runs okay?" the older woman asked sarcastically.

"I'm not sure," Maggie said, feigning ignorance. "I just figured when I started smelling that odor, I should stop and not go anywhere. Do you have any idea what it might be?"

"Well, if there are no warning lights on the dashboard, why don't you get back in and try driving it?"

"Are you sure that's a good idea?" Maggie asked.

"I know it would get you out of my way," Doris

said. "I have places to go. Just get in your car and move so I can get by."

"Okay, sorry for bothering you," Maggie said, annoyed by the woman's attitude. She returned to her car and, putting on a good performance, she slowly turned left. In her mirror, she could see Doris tossing her head around in frustration. She sped down the road, heading toward the antique store.

Maggie decided not to head back to Dogwood Mountain right away. According to the internet, at least four more antique stores listed a Hunter Springs address. She passed two that were closed and pulled into the parking lot of the third address she found.

Instead of asking questions, Maggie decided to simply browse. Like the first antique store, this one had also once been a home. She walked up the long steps to a narrow front porch. The two-story house was wide enough to accommodate several families. She wondered if the place had been a row of town-homes at one point.

A single bell jingled when she opened the wooden front door. She stepped inside and looked for a sales-person to greet her. When no one came, Maggie began browsing through the antique dressers in the front part of the store. She walked into another room, surprised to see dozens of wooden doors stacked against a wall.

"It's a little crazy, isn't it?" a voice said from behind her. She turned around to find a man standing about ten feet away. "I had no idea when I got into selling antiques that doors could be such a hot item."

"I had no idea, either," she said. "I'm Maggie. Are you the owner here?"

"Oh, no," the man said. "My name is Mark Cagle. My mother is the owner, but her advanced age makes it difficult to run the store day-to-day like she used to. She still shows up here a couple times a week to keep an eye on me."

"It's nice to meet you," Maggie said.

"Well, if there's anything I can help you with, please let me know," Mark said. "Right now, I have a set of older ladies in the back quibbling over China sets. I'll be around." He nodded his head and strolled out of the room.

Maggie browsed the doors and headed into the room across the hall. She was pleased to find around a dozen glass front curio cabinets filled with figurines. "Now we're getting somewhere," she said. She looked inside the glass cabinet, seeing multiple figurines depicting Mother Goose nursery rhyme characters. Several appeared new and brightly colored. She counted five Little Bo Peeps, seven Humpty Dumpty statues, eight figurines of Mother Goose herself, and a few others.

"You have to ask before you can get to those," a woman entered the room and said. "They don't look too kindly on strangers just opening the glass and helping themselves."

"I wasn't going to do that," Maggie said. She was certain the woman speaking to her was Linda from the yard sale. "Are you a collector?"

"A collector? I guess you could say that," Linda said. "Hey, don't I know you from somewhere?"

"Maybe," Maggie said, thinking fast. "I own a business here and in Dogwood Mountain. Maybe you saw me there."

"What business is that?" Linda said, narrowing her eyes at Maggie.

"Donut shops," Maggie blurted the words out before she thought twice. "I mean, I own a donut shop here in Hunter springs and one in Dogwood Mountain."

"Maybe that's where I've seen you before," Linda said unconvincingly. "Although, I'm not much of a fan of donuts."

"They aren't for everyone." Maggie immediately wanted to kick herself for making such a lame comment. "Anyway, enjoy shopping." She turned her back to the woman and pretended to study another set of figurines.

"Hello, again," Mark said, entering the room with Maggie. "Is there anything I can help you find in here?"

"Actually, yes." She scanned the curio cabinet for a moment, then pointed to a faded, dusty figurine in the back. "I want that one."

"Very well," Mark said. He pulled a set of keys from his pocket and unlocked the door. Carefully, he picked up the figurine between his thumb and ring finger. "This is a nice one. Forty dollars."

"Alright," Maggie said. "Shall we go up front?"

Linda watched intently as Maggie followed Mark through the room and into the front of the store. He produced an iPad from a small shelf and after a few taps on the screen, he asked for her credit card and swiped it in the attachment.

"Would you like a receipt?"

Maggie accepted her card and smiled. "Yes, please."

Mark held up his finger and left the room for a moment.

"What have you got there?" Linda crossed the

room and asked. "You should let me see that. I'm a bit of an expert on figurines."

"Oh, no," Maggie said. "I'm not worried about it. I'm in a hurry anyway." She waved dismissively hoping it was enough. Visions of the yard sale the day before danced in her brain. She clutched the figurine close to her, then decided to drop it into her handbag.

"Really, though," Linda said brightly. "Show it to me. I'm interested. I hadn't gotten around to looking in that display case just yet."

"Here we are," Mark said as he walked back toward the front. He handed a piece of paper to Maggie. "I really should move my printer up front. It would be much more convenient."

"Thank you for everything." She nodded at Linda and headed straight out the door.

Maggie was almost to her car when she heard the door chime ring. She looked over and spotted Linda heading straight for her. "Hold on a minute," Linda said. She smiled sweetly, but her eyes were narrowed.

"I'm really sorry, but I'm in a hurry," Maggie called as she opened her car door and climbed inside.

"Just wait a minute," Maggie could hear Linda shout through the car windows. She reached the car and pulled up on the door handle on the passenger door. "Roll down your window."

"No, thank you." She gently shifted the car into reverse and began slowly backing out. She hoped Linda would simply let go and step away.

"I told you to wait," Linda said, pounding on the window glass as the car slowly backed up. "Let me see that figurine. You don't know if you've gotten something rare or not. I want to see it."

Despite the woman's persistence, Maggie backed up without further incident. Linda finally gave up and stood with her hands planted on her hips, brooding at her. Maggie responded with a gentle wave, but she pressed down on the accelerator as soon as she was safely away from the older woman.

CHAPTER SEVEN

Maggie called Brett the minute she was safely away from Linda. "Something strange is definitely going on."

"I'm afraid to ask what you're referring to," Brett said. "You do remember what we talked about."

"Of course, I remember, honey," Maggie said. "I came up to Hunter Springs to meet with Bradley, but he had to cancel last minute."

"Is everything okay with him?" Brett asked.

"Yes, he's fine. He said something about taking Suzan out for a special dinner," Maggie said. Although she had interesting news to share with her husband, she wanted to stay on the topic at hand.

"Why aren't we watching Wyatt then?" The disappointment was evident in his voice.

"Because Suzan's sister is babysitting."

"What kind of a special dinner?" Brett asked.

Maggie sighed and smiled. She wasn't going to get away with withholding the information from Brett. "I think he's going to ask her to marry him," she said calmly, even though she was about to burst. "I don't know why he chose tonight, but everything worked out for them to leave the kids with Suzan's sister."

"I can't believe this is happening," Brett said. Maggie was immediately touched by his warmth toward her son. "Who knows? In another year or two we might have more grandbabies. We're gaining a new one as soon as they get married as it is."

"I know, I've been thinking about that, too," Maggie said. She hesitated before she changed the subject. "Brett, I have something to tell you. I visited a couple of antique stores here in Hunter Springs."

"What happened?" Brett asked. If he was upset with her, it didn't show.

"For one thing, I have a little better understanding about the value of these silly figurines," Maggie said, glancing at the package in her handbag. "Apparently, collections of them can fetch quite a surprising amount of money."

"Don't tell me you picked one up."

"I did, as a matter of fact," Maggie said, chuckling softly. "I spent forty whole dollars on it, but that's where things got interesting. I saw two of the women that were at the yard sale yesterday."

"Did they recognize you?" Brett asked.

"Thankfully, no," Maggie said. "Especially since I pretended my car was messed up just to get a good glimpse of the first one."

"You do know that might have blown up in your face."

"I know, but it didn't," Maggie said. "Anyway, at the second store, I ran directly into the other one. Remember how they acted toward Janine at the yard sale? That's exactly what she did to me. She even followed me out to my car and pounded on the passenger window as I backed out of the parking space. It was insane."

"Are you sure? I mean, you're sure it was one of the same women?"

"Completely sure," Maggie said. "Doris was the first woman and Linda was the second."

"And you're positive that she wanted to talk to you about the figurine you bought?" Brett said.

"Yes, absolutely sure," Maggie said, growing irritated at his questioning. "That's all she asked me about. She demanded to see it because she said she hadn't had the chance to look over the figurines in the display case where I found this one. She was adamant and relentless."

"As outrageous as all of this is, it still doesn't mean any of those women had something to do with Janine's death," Brett reminded her.

"I know," Maggie said. "I'm quite aware that what I experienced proves nothing."

"I wouldn't say it proves nothing, but it certainly doesn't prove they had anything to do with her death. It does, however, cast suspicion on them and their behavior at the yard sale."

"Does that mean you plan to pursue this?" Maggie asked carefully.

"No, not at all. This isn't my investigation," Brett said quickly. "What I plan to do is call Brooks as soon as we get off the phone and fill him in on what happened. It will be up to him whether his department decides to look into this any further."

"Something just isn't right with all of this," Maggie said. "I don't know what Brooks is going to find out, but I do hope he looks into it."

"And if he doesn't?"

"I'm not sure," Maggie admitted. "I'm not much for antiques, and I'm not sure what more I can do beyond what I've already done. I guess at the end of the day, I have an old figurine to keep me company."

"I have one more question for you," Brett said. "Where do you plan to put that figurine? Because I really don't want it looking down on me when I'm trying to sit and enjoy something on television."

"You haven't even seen it yet." Maggie laughed.

"True, but there's something I've never told you before. I was afraid of Mother Goose when I was a child," Brett said. "If it were up to me, you wouldn't even bring that thing in the house."

After trying really hard not to make fun of her husband, Maggie ended the call and concentrated on the drive ahead. Her mind drifted back to the conversation she'd had with her son. For all she knew, any minute now, her phone would ring, and he would tell her whether or not Suzan accepted his proposal. She felt a gentle thrill rush over her. A wedding was such a happy occasion, and, unlike his first wedding, this one promised to be much more stable.

When she arrived home at last, Maggie decided to leave the figurine wrapped up just as she had received it from Mark at the antique store. She hid it in her bag to avoid terrifying Brett and kept her phone right next to her for the remainder of the evening.

Just before nine o'clock, her phone rang. "It's

Bradley," she said excitedly. She picked up the phone and held it to her ear. "Hi, honey."

"Mom," Bradley said. "She said yes! Suzan and I are getting married."

Maggie covered the phone with her hand and turned to Brett who was waiting in the hallway. "Bradley asked Suzan to marry him, and he just called to tell me she said yes."

"Atta boy," Brett said, pumping his fist in the air.

"Brett is really excited for you," Maggie said. "I'm so happy for you, too, Bradley. Congratulations, sweetheart."

"Listen, I have to go," Bradley said. "I left Suzan at the table, but I just wanted to call and tell you. We are so excited."

Maggie ran straight for Brett. "I'm so happy for him," she said when he circled her in his arms. "After everything he's been through, raising Wyatt on his own, everything… This is just wonderful news."

Brett squeezed tighter and kissed her on top of her forehead. When she headed for bed a little while later, her mind was filled with thoughts of wedding dresses and suits for small ring bearers. Gone was any concern over small statues, Janine Lawrence, and the four women who harassed her before her death.

CHAPTER EIGHT

"Why are you smiling so loudly this morning?" Orson asked, holding his hand over his eyes. "Because I can tell you it's already on my last nerve."

"Good morning to you, too, sunshine," Maggie said. She placed a fresh mug of coffee in front of the cranky old man and waited for his response.

"I guess you can keep smiling," Orson said, lifting the mug off of the prep table and taking a sip. "What's got you in such a good mood this morning?"

"I think the real question is why are you in such a bad mood this morning?" Myra asked him and rolled her eyes.

"I don't want to talk about it," Orson snapped.

"Someone decided to stay out all night," Myra

smirked. "He's grumpier when he's tired, if you can believe it."

"I did no such thing. I was home by midnight, Mother." Orson scowled. "Gretchen and I were watching movies and that's the last I'm going to say about it."

"I wasn't aware one could smile too loudly," Maggie whispered to Myra. The pair giggled as they walked together into the storage room.

"Seriously, why are you so happy this morning?" Myra asked. "The last I knew you were getting wrapped up in the details of that lady who died."

"Oh, I'm still wrapped up in that," Maggie said. "I just had some good news last night. That's all."

"Don't tell me," Myra said, clasping her hands together. "It has to do with your son, doesn't it?"

"What has to do with your son?" Ruby called from the kitchen.

"I'll make an announcement when we're all together," Maggie said. She gathered the ingredients she needed for her first batch of cinnamon rolls and headed back into the kitchen. Naomi walked through the back door as she set the flour canister down on the baker's table.

"Good morning, everyone," Naomi said.

"Be quiet," Orson demanded. "Maggie was about to make an announcement."

"Okay," Naomi said. "What's going on?"

"Yes, please, fill us in," Ruby said eagerly.

"Bradley called me last night and said he'd asked Suzan to marry him and that she said yes." She was immediately swept up in a group hug with the other women. Orson remained on his stool with his eyes covered. "Orson? Is something wrong?"

"Oh, no, not a thing," Orson said. He swiped his hand over his eyes. "That is really wonderful news, Maggie. Congratulations." He pushed himself off the wooden stool and shuffled slowly toward her. He wrapped his arms around her and planted a kiss on her cheek.

"Thank you," Maggie said. Her voice was filled with emotion.

"I don't mean to change the subject," Ruby said. "But I'm really curious if you figured out anything about those figurines?"

"As a matter of fact, I did." Maggie quickly filled them in on the events in Hunter Springs.

"It sounds like something more is going on to me," Naomi said. "Do you think the stores you went to are relevant in some way?"

"Honestly, I have no idea," Maggie said. "I suppose it's possible."

"What if someone around here got a tip about a rare figurine that was posted in one of those online groups we talked about?" Naomi said.

"You think that's why those ladies are so interested in every figurine they see?" Maggie asked.

"I'm not sure, but I bet they're convinced where there's one, there's more," Naomi said.

"I suppose they're making their way through the Ozarks in search of those pieces," Maggie said. "I guess that makes sense."

"These people do it all the time," Naomi said.

"I was thinking," Myra said. "If you have access to any of those online groups, could you browse through and see if anyone has mentioned this area?"

"That's not a bad idea," Naomi said. "Maybe I'll do that later on my break."

"Speaking of a break," Orson cut in. "You ladies might want to stop gabbing and start baking. You have less than an hour before the doors open."

"You know, Orson," Ruby said. "I think you spend more time in this kitchen on that stool than you ever did while you were still employed here."

"Let's be honest," Myra said. "He never stopped working here."

"That's right. I'm your manager emeritus," Orson said.

"It basically means he's our manager forever," Ruby said, smirking at Orson. "He won't quit or be fired."

"Sounds about right to me," Orson said.

Maggie added six more donuts to the count she planned to make of the new Kitchen Sink donut. "Keep those back here," she said to Myra while they prepared the others for the display case. "Those are for Orson."

"All six? Do you think he'll eat all of these?" Myra asked.

"Hopefully not in one sitting like he did yesterday," Maggie said as she pushed her way through the swinging door to the dining area.

Once they opened, Maggie floated between the kitchen and the front helping where she could.

"Maggie, could you come here for a moment?" Naomi whispered around ten. She stood in the doorway between the kitchen and the dining room.

"Sure, what's up?" Maggie asked. She made her way to the door, expecting Naomi to turn around and head back into the dining room. She was confused when Naomi held the door closed.

"I need you to take a peek at the table left of the front door," Naomi said. "Don't let them see you."

"What's going on?" Maggie asked.

"Just look," Naomi said. She moved out of Maggie's way and waited while she cracked the door and looked. "Do you see them?"

Maggie scanned the room for a second before her eyes rested on the table Naomi mentioned. As soon as she spotted them, she held her breath for a second. All four women from the yard sale were seated at one of her tables. "That's them," she said, closing the door again. "Did they order anything?"

"No, they didn't even come up to the counter," Naomi said. "They just walked in and sat down."

"Who are you guys talking about?" Ruby asked.

"It's the four women from the yard sale," Maggie said.

"They're out there right now?" Ruby asked.

"Yeah, they just came in and sat down without saying a word," Naomi said.

"I suppose we ought to go deal with that then," Ruby said.

"What are you going to do?" Maggie asked.

"I'm just going to ask them if they would like something to eat or some coffee," Ruby said.

"And if they refuse?" Maggie asked.

"I'll tell them in order to occupy any space in the donut shop, they need to be paying customers," she said with a smile. "We've been hopping all morning because of the citywide yard sale. There are more customers in the lobby right now than we have seating. They will either understand or they will have to leave."

Ruby pushed her way through the swinging door, not waiting for a response. Naomi glanced at Maggie, then returned to the door and pushed it open to watch. Maggie joined her, not wanting to miss a bit of it.

"Good morning, ladies," Ruby said to the four women. "Is there anything I can help you with?"

"No, thank you," Doris said.

"Would you like some coffee, or maybe some donuts?" Ruby continued.

"No, we just wanted to come in and sit down for a little while," another woman replied.

"I'm sure you can see we're full here," Ruby said, gesturing around the room. "You're welcome to stay as long as you order something, but we're unable to accommodate people who are not paying customers. I'm sure you understand."

"No, I don't think we do understand," Linda piped up and said. "I would like to see your manager."

"I am the manager," Ruby said. "Not to mention,

the co-owner. I assure you I am in full authority to tell you to either order or move on."

"Boy, talk about small town service," Linda said, rather loudly. "Imagine telling four elderly women they can't come in out of the heat and take a breather without ordering something from the menu." Her volume increased with each word.

"I've got to go out there and put an end to this," Maggie said to Naomi. "She's not going to stop until she causes a scene."

"What makes you think that's what they want?" Naomi asked.

"That's the one I ran into at the antique store," Maggie explained. "I made the mistake of telling her I owned a donut shop in Dogwood Mountain." She pushed through the swinging door and headed straight for the table.

"And just who are you?" Doris asked when Maggie approached. "Hey, wait a minute. You look familiar."

"I'm the other owner of this donut shop," Maggie declared. "My business partner has been more than kind. Please order from the menu or move along."

"Hey, remember me?" Linda said. "We met at the antique store yesterday."

"Which antique store?" the fourth woman asked.

"Cagle's Antiques," Linda said quickly.

"I don't think that was the only one you were at yesterday, was it?" Doris asked. "I think you're the lady I saw outside the Olbermann store, aren't you?"

"Okay, ladies," Ruby cut in. "What business is it of yours whether she was at an antique store or not?"

"I think she knows," Linda said, eyeing Maggie.

"This is your last warning," Ruby said calmly. "Either go up to the counter and order or leave."

Doris opened her mouth to say something but shut it quickly. Maggie turned to the right, just in time to see Brett walk into the donut shop in full uniform. She glanced sideways at the table of women before leaving Ruby's side and heading straight toward Brett. "Good morning, sweetheart," she said, loud enough for the women to hear her. "Would you like something to eat?"

"You bet," Brett said, bending over to kiss her on the cheek. "Is everything okay?"

"I think we better be moving on, girls," Doris stood up suddenly and said.

"Yeah, let's get out of here," Linda agreed, hurrying everyone out.

"That uniform worked like a charm," Orson said as soon as the women left. He carried his coffee mug with him to the counter. "I just want you to know I was watching everything."

"I'm sure you were," Brett said. He patted Orson on the shoulder.

"No, I mean it," Orson said. "If they had started any trouble, I was right there."

"While I appreciate knowing that I can count on you to keep the ladies safe, I'd like to know what they were doing here," Brett said.

"I'm not sure about that part, but you know, it's almost like I'm a hero or something," Orson said.

"What are you getting at?" Ruby asked Orson.

"Well, some places treat heroes rather special." His gaze shifted to the display case.

"Maggie already put six of them on a plate in the back for you," Ruby said.

"That's why she's my favorite." He winked at her and headed through the swinging door into the kitchen after his donuts.

"What are we going to do with him?" Ruby asked, shaking her head.

"What are we going to do with any of you?" Brett said. "The last thing I expected to see when I walked in here was those four women. What were they doing here?"

"No clue," Maggie said.

"Why don't we go in the back and have this discussion?" Ruby suggested.

"Good idea," Maggie said, pulling Brett by his hand through the door into the kitchen. As soon as they walked in, Orson held up his plate of donuts, offering one to Brett.

"Thank you," Brett said, accepting a donut.

"Don't thank me," Orson said with his mouth full. "Your wife is trying to make me fat."

"What were those women doing here?" Brett asked again, ignoring Orson's comment.

"They just showed up and sat down," Naomi said. "They wouldn't order or anything."

"They were here because they know Maggie works here," Ruby said.

"Is that true?" Brett asked Maggie.

"I'm afraid so," Maggie said, shivering slightly. "They started asking me why I was at the antique stores yesterday."

"What else did they say?" Brett said.

"You walked in before they had a chance to say much," Ruby said. "Based on what they did say, though, I don't think they're up to any good."

CHAPTER NINE

"I'll stay a little later this afternoon," Maggie said to Ruby the next day. "I've taken off enough early afternoons that I owe you one."

"That isn't necessary, but it will make it easier for me to meet with a certain young couple determined to get married on my farm." Ruby grinned.

"Bradley and Suzan are coming out today?" Maggie felt her spirit soar at the mention of her son and soon-to-be daughter-in-law. "Are they bringing the kids?"

"That's the plan," Ruby said. "Apparently, neither Suzan nor her daughter have ever visited a farm before."

"That should be interesting," Naomi said. "I'll

stay behind and work with Maggie so you can take off."

"Only if you're sure."

"Of course, we are," Maggie said. She cast a sideways look at Naomi. "Besides, the two of us might have some more sleuthing to do this afternoon."

An hour after they locked the door for the day, Naomi followed Maggie outside into the alley. She waited as Maggie turned the key in the back door lock. "I had a thought."

"Tell me."

"I know this is sort of your domain, and I didn't get a chance to check it out yesterday, but I thought I might spend part of the evening going through some of those online discussion groups. You know, the ones who post about antiques and collectibles? I think I'm going to get comfortable and spend some time looking through them for any mention of this area."

"What do you think you'll find?" Maggie asked.

"Probably nothing, but I have the time and the curiosity. If I find anything useful, I'll be sure to report it to Brooks."

"I think that's a very good idea." Maggie said. "Be sure to let me know what you find, too."

They parted ways and Maggie drove the short

distance home. She thought about Naomi's idea and found herself instantly relieved that Naomi had decided to take on the task of sorting through pages of discussions for any mention of figurines or their part of the Ozarks. Brett had informed her at breakfast he planned to work late to finish up some trivial paper-work, so Maggie planned to take advantage of the alone time to relax with some wine and a movie.

Just before dark, she glanced at the clock and wondered how the meeting between her son and Ruby had gone. She hoped the meeting would mean a date would be quickly set for the wedding. She looked for her phone, in case Ruby had left her a message, but it was nowhere to be found.

Maggie rolled her eyes at herself when she real-ized her cell phone was still sitting on her desk in the office at the donut shop. She grabbed her keys and rushed outside to her car. She pulled up behind the back door and opened it quickly, flipping on the lights as she went inside. Just as she thought, her cell phone was right where she'd left it, next to her laptop.

On her way back outside, Maggie scrolled through a series of messages. She squealed with delight when she spotted a message from Bradley himself. "Save the date," he wrote. "We have decided on an October seventh wedding. Hope you can make it." The message was followed by a series of laughing emojis.

"I'll check my schedule and get back to you," she replied and laughed. "Congratulations to you both."

She turned to lock the door behind her when she felt the hair stand up on the back of her neck. She looked up and down the alley, straining to focus under the dim lights above. When she saw nothing, she walked back to her car. Her phone chimed, indicating another text message. She paused at her car door and looked at the screen. Before she could open the message, she heard someone behind her. As she turned around, something slipped over her head and the world around her went black.

"Let me go," Maggie screamed. Her arms flailed around her head as she attempted to fight off whomever had placed the hood over her eyes. Her hands connected with something, but it did her no good. She felt two arms circling her neck, pulling her backwards. She was dragged to the ground beside her car. She felt a blow to her upper back, as if someone had driven their knee into her back. "What do you want?"

"I want what you got at the antique store,"

someone whispered in the darkness. "That's all I wanted from you, but you had to make things harder for me."

"I know who you are," Maggie said. The person gripped the collar of her shirt and pulled it back. Maggie felt a slight sting on her shoulder, then nothing. She reached for the hood over her face and pulled it off, when she looked around, no one was in the alley with her.

Maggie exhaled heavily and gripped the side of her car to help herself to her feet. She pulled herself up, but the world spun around her, and she fell back on the ground. She lost her grip on her phone and watched helplessly as it skipped away from her. Her face was flush and hot. Her heart thundered in her chest and her fingers tingled.

"Help me," she whispered. She felt herself fall to the side. She landed on her shoulder and rolled to her back, gasping for air. She closed her eyes and tried to force herself to think. Where was her phone? Despite the pain shooting down both of her arms, she patted the ground until her fingers touched the screen. Maggie pushed her fingers into the phone and pulled it toward her. She tapped the screen and dialed 911.

When she woke up, lights burned overhead. She

looked around the small room and realized that Brett was seated next to her bed. His eyes were red and swollen.

"You're in the emergency room," he told her.

"What happened?" Maggie asked.

"I was hoping you could tell me," Brett said. "Paramedics found you lying in the alley next to your car."

"Someone attacked me," Maggie said. "I think I know who it was."

"They injected you with something," Brett continued. Maggie was confused by his lack of concern over her statement. "Nitroglycerin, to be precise. It sent your body into a tizzy."

"Are you serious?" Maggie asked.

"You're lucky that you're relatively young and healthy," the nurse on the other side of the room said. Maggie focused on her for the first time. "The dose you were given could have killed you."

"Is that how Janine died?" she asked, looking at Brett.

"That's what we're thinking," Brett said. "I called Brooks to let him know what was going on. He's searching for the women as we speak. They have some serious questions to answer."

"Do you have any idea where they are?" Maggie asked. Her eyes fluttered. She was groggy and her head pounded.

"We're doing everything we can to find them," Brett said. His jaw tightened. "You said you know who attacked you. Who was it?"

"It was the one named Linda."

"How sure are you?" Brett asked.

"Positive," she said.

"How do you know?"

"I know because she mentioned the figurine I bought at the antique store in Hunter Springs," Maggie said. She turned to face him. "Brett, you have to call the coroner. That's how she did it!"

"That's how who did what?" the nurse asked. She stood in front of a computer monitor typing in notes about Maggie's condition.

"The person who attacked me," Maggie said. "Another woman died, and I think I know how. She was injected, too. Only it was too much for her body."

"This woman, was she older? Have a heart condition?" the nurse asked.

"Yes, and yes," Brett said. "Why do you ask?"

"It's hard to say without knowing her condition," the nurse said. "But if she was sick and frail enough, and already possibly on the medication, there's a shot it was too much for her body to handle. As you said before, your wife is lucky she's young and healthy."

"I don't like this one bit," Brett said, getting up to make a call.

CHAPTER TEN

"I suppose I owe you an apology now," Brett said a few hours later, eyeing his wife.

"What do you mean?" Maggie said.

"You were the one who insisted there was something more to Janine Lawrence's death all along," he explained. "And you were right."

"Was it just Linda?" Maggie asked. "Or were all of them in on it?"

"Unless the other three ladies are very good actors, it was Linda who was responsible for killing Janine and trying to kill you," Brett said. His jaw tightened again. "I wish I had listened to you, honey,"

"I may have been wrong just as easily," Maggie said. "You were doing your job."

"I know, but I should have given you more credit

in the first place," Brett said. "As it is, we have a big mess to unravel. We're still not sure about motive, and Mrs. Cagle isn't talking."

"Mrs. Cagle? That's Linda's name? Linda Cagle," Maggie asked, repeating herself.

"Yes. Does the name mean something to you?" Brett leaned against the corner of his desk.

"I'm afraid so," Maggie said. "I'd really like to talk to Naomi about what she found online when she was looking."

"I spoke with Naomi," Brett said. "She wanted me to tell you that she found something a little fishy about the citywide yard sale."

"Really? What did she find?" Maggie asked. "I mean, the city of Dogwood Mountain legitimately hosts this event every year."

"Not about the yard sale itself," Brett said. "Something about going hard looking for hidden treasure. She thinks it's code for something."

"I think I know what that might be code for," Maggie said.

"I am all ears," Brett said. "If there's anything you know that might help us figure out this mess, I'm open to listening."

"When I was in Hunter Springs, I met a woman who owns one of the antique stores, Opal Olbermann of Olbermann Antiques," Maggie began. "She was the kind of woman who looks down on everyone around her, but she knows her antiques. She told me how valuable figurines like the Mother Goose one can be. And she also told me she keeps those collectibles in her store under lock and key."

"Under lock and key? Isn't that a bit extreme?" Brett asked.

Maggie shrugged. "People talk about a black market for this stuff, so no, I don't think it's extreme. I'll admit that I don't fully understand it, but some people really take this seriously." She sighed and leaned forward in her seat. "There's something else, too. When I went to the second antique store, I met a man named Mark Cagle. He didn't seem as worried about the figurines being rare or popular or anything."

"I'm curious if you're more concerned about his name matching Linda's or the fact that he didn't feel the same way about the figurines as some crazed collector."

"I'm concerned about them both, honestly. I think it's pretty likely that Mark is related to Linda. Especially since he mentioned his mother when I was there. He said her health kept her from running the store day-to-day. Brett, what if she had a heart condition and took nitroglycerin?"

"Didn't you say Linda was at the store that day? Why wouldn't she have introduced herself as the owner?" Brett asked.

"I have no idea, but this is the best lead so far, don't you think?"

He stood up suddenly. "You're right. I've got to go." He turned to rush out of the room and then looked back at her. "I'm sorry, honey. Can you call Ruby for a ride?"

"Where are you going?" Maggie asked.

"To Hunter Springs," Brett said firmly. "I would like to have a discussion with one Mark Cagle."

Maggie steadied herself and walked slowly down the hall after she called Ruby. She was eager to get home and get into bed. Sleeping sounded like the best remedy for her pounding head. She walked past the interview room, and headed out the back way instead of through the front where she knew she might run into someone she knew. Avoiding interaction was her first priority.

"I didn't do it," a voice called out to her. Maggie looked up in time to see Doris in handcuffs. One of Brett's deputies was leading her toward the county jail, which was attached to the Sheriff's Office. "None of us knew what Linda had planned."

"Keep it moving," the deputy said.

"Please, you have to believe me," Doris continued. "None of the other girls or I knew anything about murder. We didn't mean for that woman to die, either. Until a few minutes ago, I had no idea what Linda had done."

"Then why did you harass that poor woman?" Maggie asked. "And why did Linda come after me?"

"We're thieves," Doris shouted. "That's it. That's all. We find valuable collectibles anyway we can and then sell them. It's simple, really. When someone finds a collectible in one area, there's a good chance other pieces of the collection are in the same area."

"That doesn't make you a thief," Maggie said.

"No, it doesn't," Doris continued. The deputy stood by silently as she spoke. "But stealing valuable pieces does."

"Then why was she so interested in the little figurine I bought?" Maggie asked.

"Because one of the ways we get away with it is by hiding the merchandise in plain sight," Doris said. "That piece you picked up yesterday? That one is the real thing. Linda stole it from a collector in Little Rock three months ago. She and her son put those pieces on display to throw off the authorities, but the intention is to never sell them. Her son made a mistake when he sold that one to you."

"So, that's why she came after me?" Maggie said.

"That and the fact that you were getting too close," Doris said. "After we met your husband at the donut shop, the rest of us were content to let this go, but not Linda. Linda never lets anything go."

CHAPTER ELEVEN

"October seventh? That's when they're getting married?" Brooks asked Maggie later that week. They were seated around the bonfire at Ruby's house, discussing Bradley's impending nuptials. "That will be a wonderful time of year to get married here." Brooks looked at the land around the barn.

"I hope they have an evening wedding," Myra said, gazing wistfully at Brooks. "It's so pretty here in the silvery moonlight."

"I just hope they have the good sense to go through with it before it gets too cold," Orson grumbled. "Old men like me have no business out here when it's rainy and cold."

"They aren't holding the wedding outside, Orson," Ruby said.

"Maybe not the wedding," Orson said. "But that boy needs a bachelor party. Where do you think that's going to take place?"

"I don't know," Maggie said, cutting in. "You may have to ask his best man."

"Who's that?" Brett asked. He shifted slightly in his seat. Wyatt was asleep on his chest. Bradley and Suzan had taken off nearly an hour before on a walk around the property.

"That will depend entirely upon you," Bradley said, holding Suzan's hand as they walked up to Brett from behind.

"You're back," Brett said. "Isn't this place beautiful at night?"

"It really is," Suzan agreed. "But I think you're missing something important."

"What am I missing around here?" Ruby asked.

"Not you." Suzan laughed. "I'm talking about Brett. Bradley wants him to be the best man."

"You want me?" Brett asked, his voice shaking. "What about Zeke? Isn't he your best friend?"

"I plan to make Zeke one of my groomsmen," Bradley said. "But the best man position is reserved for someone who is even closer to me than he is."

Maggie beamed at her son and her husband. In the years that had passed since Bradley left the Navy and settled down close by, she had seen the bond between stepfather and stepson strengthen.

Brett leaned forward, hugging the sleeping boy in his arms closer to his chest. "Thank you."

"Well, I think that's your answer," Brooks said.

"Did Bradley tell you we're planning to add to our family right away?" Suzan said suddenly.

"No, he said nothing about that," Maggie said. She smiled warmly and stood up to embrace her new daughter-in-law-to-be. They were moving quickly, but it felt right.

"We wondered if you would help us decorate the nursery when the time comes," Bradley said.

"Of course, I'll help," Maggie said. She reached out to hug her son. When she released him from her embrace, she was surprised to hear the low rumble of giggles around the circle. She turned around. Naomi and Myra covered their mouths to hold in their laughter. Even grumpy Orson had a smile on his face. "What is it? What am I missing?"

"I think what they're trying to say is they want you to decorate the nursery with a particular theme in mind," Naomi said.

"Okay, I'm open to anything they want," Maggie said, looking back at Suzan and Bradley. She was growing more confused by the second.

"You might not feel that way when you find out what they want," Ruby said.

"I'm sure I'll be okay with whatever they pick," Maggie said. "What do you have in mind?"

Orson stood up suddenly. He slapped his knee and threw back his head "Oh, for Pete's sake, will someone just say it?" he shouted. "They want the baby's room to be decorated in a Mother Goose theme." He shook his head, rolled his eyes, and plopped back down on his chair. The low rumble of chuckles exploded into a round of raucous laughter.

AUTHOR'S NOTE

I'd love to hear your thoughts on my books, the storylines, and anything else that you'd like to comment on—reader feedback is very important to me. My contact information, along with some other helpful links, is listed on the next page. If you'd like to be on my list of "folks to contact" with updates, release and sales notifications, etc.... just shoot me an email and let me know. Thanks for reading!

Also…

… if you're looking for more great reads, Summer Prescott Books publishes several popular series by outstanding Cozy Mystery authors.

CONTACT SUMMER PRESCOTT BOOKS PUBLISHING

Blog and Book Catalog: http://summerprescottbooks.com
Email: summer.prescott.cozies@gmail.com

And…be sure to check out the Summer Prescott Cozy Mysteries fan page and Summer Prescott Books Publishing Page on Facebook – let's be friends!

To sign up for our fun and exciting newsletter, which will give you opportunities to win prizes and swag, enter contests, and be the first to know about New Releases, click here: http://summerprescottbooks.com

Made in United States
North Haven, CT
10 October 2023

42585471R00064